Marco's Monster

To Caroline —
With hopes for
your happy future —

Meredith Ann Wilke.

Marco's Monster

MEREDITH SUE WILLIS

HarperCollins*Publishers*

Library of Congress Cataloging-in-Publication Data
Willis, Meredith Sue.
Marco's monster / by Meredith Sue Willis.
  p.   cm.
Summary: Fourth-grader Marco has his hands full when his best friend
is chosen to be star of the class play and his little sister is accused of killing
a gerbil in her kindergarten class.
ISBN 0-06-027195-7. — ISBN 0-06-027196-5 (lib. bdg.)
[1. Schools—Fiction.   2. Brothers and sisters—Fiction.   3. Plays—
Fiction.   4. City and town life—Fiction.]   I. Title.
PZ7.W68317Mar   1996   96-14606
[Fic]—dc20   CIP
                                                               AC

2   3   4   5   6   7   8   9   10
❖
First Edition

This book is dedicated to four of Joel's cousins:

Jennie Geller Weinberger

Leah Geller Weinberger

Alex Kato-Willis

Nathan Geller Weinberger

Contents

Contents

1

MARCO AND THE SCHOOL PLAY

When I was small, I discovered I had special powers. I could fly until my mother threw away my little red cape, and last year, back when Tyrone was still a bully, I looked out my window and shrank him with my bare eyes. I never told him I did that, but he stopped being a bully, and now he's my best friend.

I don't use my special powers so much anymore. I still have Mental Sights sometimes, where I see what is going to happen before it happens. But I need my powers less now because I have a best friend and my little dog Lucy. I used to be afraid around my block, but now I am never afraid, at least when Tyrone and Lucy are with me. Tyrone and I do lots of things like play baseball on the park team and work for my Uncle Albert in his store. This year Tyrone finally learned to read. He almost never gets suspended from school. In fact, Tyrone got so good that I got mad at him.

It happened when we were working on the Monster play. Tyrone and I have Mr. Marshan this year. Mr. Marshan is a good teacher, but he gives lots of homework at night. This is to get us in shape for Fifth Grade and the Future. We get a lot of homework, but we also get to do a lot of fun things. For example, Mr. Marshan brought his camcorder into class for our special project. We could make our own videos! We had great ideas, but Lateesha and Miriam said they wanted our special project to be the Fourth Grade Play on the stage in the auditorium.

"The fourth grade always does a play," said

Lateesha. "You *have* to do a play if you're in the fourth grade. What's the use of being in the fourth grade if you do videos instead of a Fourth Grade Play?"

The boys all said, "Videos! Videos! We want videos!"

I think Mr. Marshan was on our side, but he called a class meeting, and we all sat on the rug. Personally I think sitting on a rug for class meetings is something you should do with kindergarten children like my little sister Ritzi and not with fourth graders. But Mr. Marshan says Democracy Starts with a Level Playing Field. So we sit on the rug for meetings.

Tyrone and I call the rug the Rat Skin. The rug is so dirty the custodian won't even sweep it. It has little bits of crackers and fuzz stuck in it and one big smear of something yellowish orange. No one will sit on that. If you forget and sit there, Tyrone yells, "Guinea-pig vomit! You sat in guinea-pig vomit!"

That day the boys sat on one side of the guinea-pig vomit and the girls on the other. Mr. Marshan sat down on the edge of the rug.

He was wearing his parrot tie. Mr. Marshan buys funny ties to make the class laugh. He called on Lateesha first.

Lateesha said, "The girls want our special project to be a class play just like the fourth grade always does." The girls all clapped.

The boys shouted, "No, no, we want videos! Mr. Marshan promised videos!"

Mr. Marshan said, "Now, on the rug, everyone gets his say. His or her say."

So Lateesha put her hand on her hip the way she does. "Well, this is still my say. And I say the fourth grade should do a fairy-tale play."

"A fairy tale?" said Tyrone. "A fairy tale? Boo! Boo!" Tyrone is louder and older and bigger than anyone else in the fourth grade. He has a deeper voice to make his boos, too.

All of us boys stuck together with Tyrone. We went thumbs-down. "No fairy tales!" we said. "We want videos!"

Mr. Marshan stood up. Mr. Marshan likes Democracy, but he is also a Disciplinarian. He stood there with his arms crossed over the parrot tie staring at us until it got completely quiet.

Robert raised his hand. "I'll do a fairy tale if we can do 'The Castle of Doctor Bluebeard' and cut off the girls' heads!"

The girls all yelled, "Sexist! That is so sexist!"

Lateesha said, "That is sexist *and* violent, Mr. Marshan." You could see in her eyes that she was planning on making Robert very sorry for saying that. She is almost as dangerous as Tyrone.

Mr. Marshan said, "I think we had better listen to each other politely, or there may not be a special project for this fourth grade at all."

"The girls want to do a modern fairy tale with singing and dancing," said Lateesha. "Like maybe 'Beauty and the Beast.' But we're going to do it our way! In our play the girl is very cool, and the Beast will be a monster with a whole posse of other monsters. And the monsters will fight a lot."

I looked around at the other boys. They were all looking around at each other and me. We were all thinking it didn't sound so bad after all.

Then I had a Mental Sight. It was so real, it was like a Prediction of the Future. I saw myself on the stage with spotlights. The auditorium was dark and full of little kids, and they were all screaming and squealing in fear! They were having a wonderful time.

I didn't mean to go over to Lateesha's side so easily, but a name for the play just popped up in my brain like it was written there. I said, "We could call this play 'Cool Girl and the Main Monster.'"

"Okay," said Lateesha, like it was all settled. "You could call it that. Miriam's mother is going to sew costumes, and my father is going to make monster masks for all the monsters." The masks were going to have horns and Dracula fangs, she told us. All of the Monster Posse would get monster masks, and the Main Monster would get a whole head. Well, right then, the war between the boys and girls was over. Everyone looked at Mr. Marshan and waited.

He rubbed his beard and pulled on his parrot tie. "Well," he said, "I guess we could find a way to use the camcorder too. We could make commercials for our play. We could also tape it, of course. Maybe we'll use a couple of cameras, and then we could edit the best shots together. . . ."

It was a pretty good example of Democracy after all, Mr. Marshan told us. Everyone was finding a way to get in what they wanted. Lateesha and Miriam would get to dance and lip-synch their favorite songs. The monsters would get to do scary fights. We would still use the camcorder. Mr. Marshan even had a special classic song from the Golden Oldie Days about monsters dancing in a graveyard.

We all started walking around, boys and girls both, with our arms out like Frankenstein's monster.

In my Mental Sight I had seen myself onstage, so I figured that meant I was going to be the Main Monster. He would be the most scary one of all. I had an idea for the Monster to have a dog, too. My idea was for me to play the Main Monster and to get my little dog Lucy into the play. But Mr. Marshan put off deciding who got to be the Main Monster until we had the script finished.

One week later, he called another meeting and started to give out parts. Lateesha got Cool Girl, of course, and her best friend, Miriam, got to be her best friend in the play.

He named all of the boys who got to play monsters. Everyone was waiting to see who got the Main Monster. Mr. Marshan looked at his script and blew on his glasses. "Now," he said, "we need a Narrator. Marco will be the Narrator."

I felt like you do when you are running and you fall down when you least expect it.

I said, "I don't want to be the Narrator, Mr. Marshan! I want to be the Main Monster!"

"You're a good reader, Marco," said Mr. Marshan. "I can depend on you to shout if the microphone breaks, which it does about half the time. The Narrator is a very important part."

I said, "But Mr. Marshan, I want to be the Main Monster."

"I'm not going to do the dance at the end with Marco!" said Lateesha. "Marco's too small to be the Main Monster."

Tyrone stood up and said, "I guess that means me, Mr. Marshan. I'm the biggest boy in the class. I'm the meanest, too."

Robert laughed. "Yeah, Tyrone. You're a monster all right!"

I couldn't believe it. Not one hour ago Tyrone and I were walking to school and I had told him I wanted to be the Main Monster. And he said, Sure, Marco, I guess you'll be the Main Monster. He never once said he wanted it!

Mr. Marshan looked at Tyrone and said, "I think Tyrone would make an excellent Main Monster."

"No way!" said Lateesha. "I'm not going to do the love dance at the end with Tyrone!"

"I'm not going to do it with her!" said Tyrone.

I was starting to feel like I was the most unlucky kid in the world. I said, "Give me a chance, Mr. Marshan! Sometimes the meanest monsters are the short ones!"

Lateesha said, "I'm not doing the love dance with Marco, or Tyrone either. No way."

Mr. Marshan said, "Well, Lateesha, if you refuse to dance with any of the boys, then we'll have to get a Cool Girl who will."

Lateesha shut up.

"Look at me be a monster, Mr. Marshan!" Tyrone said. He jumped up on his chair and made his face all twisted and sort of dragged one arm down low. He looked scary even without a monster head. He stretched his big arm at Lateesha, but she knocked it away. Then he started making monster noises at me. I just stared at him.

Mr. Marshan had decided: Tyrone was going to be the Main Monster. Robert and some other boys were going to wear masks and do the Monster dance. *I* had to be the stupid Narrator. I sat there thinking, This is what you get for being a good reader? You have to stand on the side of the stage and wear a tie and a sport jacket while your friends get to play monsters?

I might have finished being mad sooner, but all afternoon Tyrone kept making the monster face and growling. "I'm the Main Monster," he would say, like we were going to forget!

He monster-walked to gym, and he monster-shot baskets, and he monster-carried the balls back to the closet. He was so bigheaded, I felt like throwing up.

I finally said, "You know you won't stay the Main Monster, Tyrone. You know you'll get thrown out of the play for bad behavior."

His eyebrows went real low over his eyes and his lips stuck out, but I didn't care. I never was so mad in my whole life. I was mad at Mr. Marshan and Tyrone and Lateesha and everyone I knew.

After school, Tyrone and I always go pick up my sister. But that day I didn't wait for him. I grabbed Ritzi by the arm and made her run. I never looked back, not even when I heard Tyrone calling my name.

2
A ROTTEN POTATO

I hid behind the curtain of our living-room window and watched for Tyrone. I made my little dog Lucy stop jumping on me, and I told Ritzi to stay out of sight. After a while he came down the street. He rang the bell downstairs, but I stayed behind the curtain.

Ritzi said, "That's Tyrone."

I said, "Shut up."

"That's disrespectful," said Ritzi.

I said, "You can't be disrespectful to a kindergarten kid."

Tyrone stepped out into the street and looked up, but he didn't see me. I felt very powerful, like I could make myself invisible.

"I want a peanut-butter sandwich," said Ritzi. She doesn't eat jelly, just peanut butter, and sometimes not even bread.

"I don't care," I said. I didn't care about anything. Who cares if Ritzi's hungry? I thought. Who cares if Tyrone gets to be the Main Monster? I don't want it anyway.

Tyrone shrugged and walked away like he didn't care either. He lives down at the end of the block, where the empty buildings are, and his house doesn't look much different from the empty ones. There are certain places I'm not supposed to go ever. One is Tyrone's building. Another one is the Other Side of the Park.

Ritzi got her own peanut butter on a spoon. Then she played Operating Room with her dolls. I watched television and played with my little dog Lucy until Mama got home. I kept thinking Tyrone was yelling for me, and I would run to the window, but he was never there.

* * *

That night I had a dream about the play. In the dream I was still the Narrator of the play, but I was also part of the play. When the Main Monster came out on the stage in my dream, he was so scary he even chased the Narrator—me! I woke up with the idea, and I could hardly wait to tell someone.

I tried to tell Mama, but she had to go to work. She always gets up and walks Lucy and makes our lunches and puts out the cereal bowls and cereal boxes. Then she wakes us up and leaves. Ritzi got up and started playing with her Barbies.

I said, "Come on, Ritzi, eat your breakfast. I don't want to miss Tyrone. I have something important to tell him."

Ritzi opened up her special wallet where she keeps her Operating Instruments. I should explain that my sister Ritzi is not an ordinary little girl. She is what you call a Prodigy, which means smarter than anyone you know. I am not saying she is a Genius, but she could read the newspaper when she was three years old.

She is also not ordinary because she was

born with her heart full of holes. She had to have an operation when she was only hours old. Then she had to have another operation when she was two years old, and that time they took her kidney. Everyone else has two kidneys, but my sister Ritzi just has one. It is like she lost her kidney and got an extra brain instead. She never plays Fashion Outfits with her Barbies; she plays Operations.

She was doing an operation on her favorite Barbie, No-Arm No-Leg. You might as well call it No-Hair and Not-Much-Face-Either.

"Hurry up and eat, Ritzi," I said.

She ate about three bites of cereal and then went back to No-Arm.

"Are you finished?" I said. "I'm going to throw away the cereal." I was afraid Tyrone wouldn't wait for me, since I'd run off without him the day before.

"I'm not going to school today," said Ritzi.

Sometimes I get so tired of having a sister. "Yes you are. You have to go to school."

She shook her head. "I'm not going today."

"Don't say you're not going to school," I

said to her, "because you are going to school. So shut up about not going to school. Get your stuff and let's go."

"No-Arm No-Leg is having an appendectomy." She had out her little knife for spreading butter, a needle, and a nail file.

"I don't care about No-Brain's operation," I said. "We have to go!"

"I'm stitching her back up now."

I let her do it. Stitch stitch stitch. I said, "How come you use a real needle and imaginary thread?"

"It isn't imaginary thread; it's invisible thread."

I went over to the window and looked down, and here came Tyrone. Real fast I unlocked the window, pushed it up, and yelled through the safety bars, "Hey, Tyrone! Look up! Wait for us, Tyrone. I got to talk to you!" He didn't say anything, but he didn't walk away either.

"Hurry up, Ritzi!"

She pretended to tie a knot in the Barbie's stomach, and then she got out this old straw

bag with decorations on the side that say
WELCOME TO PUERTO RICO. She started stuffing
Barbies into it.

"You can't take the Barbies to school!" I
said.

She doesn't say much, my sister Ritzi. She
kept packing up the Barbies, and she took the
Operating Instruments wallet, too.

I was dressed, I had my hair combed, I had
my book bag and her book bag, and my lunch
and her lunch, and Tyrone was waiting. My
dog Lucy was jumping up and down, *yip yip
yip*, because this is the part of the day she
hates. I hate to leave her, too.

"Don't take the Barbies, Ritzi!" I said.

She went back and got one more.

I gave up. At least she was coming.

Outside, Tyrone said, "I was waiting a
long time for you, Marco! What happened
yesterday? I thought we were going to play
basketball."

I said, "I thought you had to work at Uncle
Albert's store."

I wanted to tell him my idea right away, but

Ritzi was walking slower and slower. "Hurry up, Ritzi," I said.

"It's heavy," she said.

"You're the one who had to bring all the Barbies!"

I said to Tyrone, "She had to take her dolls to school today. She had to take every Barbie she owns in that stupid bag. You don't know, Tyrone. You don't know what it's like to have to get some little girl dressed every morning and baby-sit her every afternoon."

"I wouldn't mind," said Tyrone. Sometimes he acts like he likes Ritzi better than me. "How come you taking the Barbies, Little Ritz?" asked Tyrone.

"This is the Mobile Intensive Care Unit."

"Hey, Tyrone," I said. "I have to tell you my idea. I know you're going to be the Main Monster in the play—"

He got this big stupid grin on his face. "I told my mother about the play," he said. "I told my mother I am the star of the play."

"You better not tell Lateesha you're the star."

"You'll see," said Tyrone. "I'll be the star. My mother is going to come to the play. She said she had to see this to believe it."

Tyrone's mother and father never come to school. They don't come for Back to School Night, and they don't come if Tyrone is in trouble. They just don't come. I think maybe Tyrone's father can't come anyway because he is in jail.

I said, "Listen to my idea. My idea is to scare the kids so bad that they think the Monster is real—"

"I won't be scared," said Ritzi.

"Yes you will," I said. "If we do my idea. It goes like this: Here's the Narrator on the side of the stage, and then here comes the Main Monster—that's you, Tyrone—"

"Yeah!" He grinned. "I'm the Main Monster all right!"

"So you get all mean, and you chase . . . me, the Narrator!"

Tyrone said, "But the Narrator isn't in the play."

"That's what makes it good! This Monster is so crazy, this Monster is so bad and dangerous, he can even chase the Narrator of the play! So I run all over the stage, and all the little kids scream and yell. And, Tyrone, get this! You chase me out into the audience!"

"That's good, Marco!" said Tyrone. "I like it. Chasing you will be fun. I was afraid you were mad. It wouldn't have been no fun if you didn't be in the play."

I was surprised. I never meant for anyone to think I wouldn't be in the play.

Not only did Mr. Marshan like my idea, he suggested the Monster could pretend to grab little kids in the audience! We talked and talked and practiced our lines. We had such a long meeting on the Rat Skin, we were almost late for our gym period. We were just putting our books away when the principal, Mrs. Gates, came in.

Mrs. Gates is very big and always wears everything the same color. That day she was purple. We got very quiet when she came in. She said something to Mr. Marshan, and he said, "Marco, go with Mrs. Gates."

First I thought, Uh-oh, what did I do? Then

I remembered the last time she came and got me. That was the last time Ritzi ran away.

"Is Ritzi okay?" I asked.

Mrs. Gates said, "Ritzi won't go inside her classroom."

I was relieved. This was nothing. "She's pretty stubborn sometimes, Mrs. Gates."

"She said she wanted to see you."

Ritzi's kindergarten is in the basement, toward the back of the school. You can look out the windows and see the custodian's feet when he puts out the garbage.

Ritzi had bad luck this year. Maybe I should say her teacher had the bad luck, because her teacher was the one who got hit by a bus. The teacher had two broken legs and a concussion. So Mrs. Gates had to get a substitute until the teacher got well.

Ritzi was sitting on the floor outside the kindergarten, sewing up a Barbie. The only difference from this morning was that now she was using invisible thread *and* an invisible needle.

Mrs. Gates said, "Good afternoon, Ritzi."

"Good afternoon, Mrs. Gates," said Ritzi. "Hi, Marco."

I said, "Ritzi, you should be in your class, not playing Barbies."

At that moment the substitute popped out the door like she had been waiting for us. Her name was Mrs. Rettle, and Ritzi didn't like her. My mother told Ritzi to be patient; her real teacher would be back soon.

Uncle Albert says never be surprised if a ten-pound bag of potatoes has a rotten one at the bottom. The way I figure it is, all the good substitutes had been picked, and at the bottom of the bag was Mrs. Rettle.

From a distance she looked pretty normal, but up close you could tell she didn't take good care of herself. Her hair was pinned up, but some pieces had fallen down. She had an okay skirt, but there were lots of little silvery hairs on it. Not just one or two hairs like when Lucy sheds, but so many hairs, it looked like her skirt was trying to turn itself into a fur coat.

She said, "Mrs. Gates! I'm so sorry to bother

you, but Ritzi caused a big scare this afternoon, isn't that right, Ritzi?"

Ritzi looked once at Mrs. Rettle, and then
she looked at Mrs. Gates and me, and then she
went back to sewing up the doll.

Mrs. Rettle said, "Ritzi chased a cat with
scissors, Mrs. Gates. I was very surprised, but I
guess in this day and age, you have to expect a
certain amount of Violence in the Schools."

"Scissors?" said Mrs. Gates. "Cat?"

"She got the scissors off my desk, but ear-
lier in the day I'd already had to take away a
box of needles and sharp instruments that she
brought to school."

"That's her operating kit," I said. "She's
going to be a doctor. She practices operations
on her Barbies."

Mrs. Gates said, "What cat are we talking
about?"

"I wouldn't hurt Big Boss," said Ritzi.

"Who," asked Mrs. Gates, "is Big Boss?"

I knew the answer to that. "He's the boss cat
that hangs around the garbage cans outside."

Mrs. Rettle said, "Those cats get in. If we

open our windows even the smallest bit for air, they walk right in." As she said this, she smiled. But her smile was like her lipstick; it didn't fit her mouth.

Mrs. Gates said, "We can't have cats coming into the school."

"I didn't let the cat in!" said Mrs. Rettle. "I don't know how the cat got in!"

I said, "My sister loves animals."

Mrs. Rettle looked down at me, and she was not smiling. "Well, so do I, little boy. I like animals too!"

Mrs. Gates said, "Ritzi, what happened with the cat?"

"Big Boss had strings around his neck. He was all wrapped up. I was going to cut the strings."

Mrs. Rettle said, "Well, you didn't tell *me* that. *I* didn't see any string. What I saw was a little girl with scissors running after a cat."

"So," said Mrs. Gates. "We have several things here. We have a cat that should not be in the classroom. We have sharp instruments brought to school that should not be brought,

Ritzi. We have *untangling* a cat. Let's take one at a time. Ritzi, you may not bring sharp things to kindergarten anymore. Right?"

"Right," said Ritzi.

"Mrs. Rettle, we must be careful about these cats. I'll be writing a memorandum to the whole school about the cats."

"They're very nice cats," said Mrs. Rettle. "But of course, no cats in the classroom!"

"Now that we've sorted this out," said Mrs. Gates, "let's pick up the dolls and go back inside."

"No," said Ritzi.

Mrs. Rettle looked at Ritzi and shook her head.

"Ritzi," said Mrs. Gates, "would you like Marco to go in with you for a while?"

I could hear my class arriving in the gym overhead. I said, "Oh, Ritzi is fine. You're fine, aren't you, Ritzi?"

"I want Marco," said Ritzi.

So I had to spend my whole gym period sitting on a little tiny chair watching the kindergarten kids do their work. When it got very boring, which was soon, I stared at the rabbit. I got sick of his twitchy little nose, so I watched the gerbils curled up and sleeping in their gerbil litter. All the time, like torture, I could hear my class playing over my head.

And Tyrone said he wouldn't mind having a little sister!

3

A GOOD AFTERNOON TURNS BAD

After that, things went okay for a while. Ritzi quit taking her Mobile Intensive Care Unit to school, and we started rehearsals for "Cool Girl and the Main Monster."

The girls practiced acting and dancing all the time. The boys practiced wearing their masks and doing the Monster dance. I added more parts for the Narrator. Then one day Lateesha's dad brought in the head for the

Main Monster. The other masks were good, but oh man, you should have seen the Main Monster!

It had fur and teeth and a black nose like a wolf and blue and yellow streaks. It had horns on top and horns in front and horns out the side. Everybody wanted to touch it, but Mr. Marshan said Tyrone first. So Lateesha's father slipped it over Tyrone's head.

Right then, Tyrone turned into the Monster. I don't mean he started acting like the Monster. He'd been acting like the Monster already. What happened was . . . he grew! Right in front of us, he grew! His shoulders raised up and he got twice as tall as he used to be. He started to walk very slowly, and very slowly he raised up his arms and looked down at us and growled. We all got quiet.

Lateesha's father laughed and laughed. He said Tyrone was a high-class Monster. He gave Tyrone a high five and a low five, and he called him Young Brother and My Man, and by the time he left, Tyrone's *real* head swelled up so much he could hardly take off the Monster head.

He said, "Let's have a rehearsal, Mr. Marshan!"

"No," said Mr. Marshan, "not till later. We have our Friday-afternoon business."

"Can I do my work with the head on?" said Tyrone. "I need to, you know, get used to it."

"No, you can't do your work with the head on," said Mr. Marshan. He made Tyrone put the head back in the plastic garbage bag. Then he made him put it in the coatroom. "We have to take good care of it," said Mr. Marshan. "It is a Work of Art."

After the head was put away, Mr. Marshan said, "Now for our Friday-afternoon business. I'd like everybody to get out their—"

Tyrone interrupted him. "Mr. Marshan! Mr. Marshan! Can I take the head home? I want to show it to somebody."

I was starting to get tired of this. I said, in a little baby voice, "He wants to show his mommy," and everybody laughed.

Tyrone said, "Are you talking about my mother, Marco?"

"That's enough," said Mr. Marshan.

"That's enough about mothers and the head, too. I want everyone to get out their pencils. Robert, you're paper monitor this week. Please pass out paper for the spelling test."

This was when the afternoon began to get bad. I had forgotten about the spelling test. Spelling is one of my pretty good subjects, but what I do is, I memorize the words right before the test. Sometimes I do it out on the playground, sometimes in the lunch room. I keep the list in my pocket, and right before the test I memorize them really quick. That way they're fresh in my brain. I usually get twenty out of twenty. But that day I had forgotten it was Friday. I never once looked at my list.

Everybody groaned like they always do, and Mr. Marshan said like he always does, "Now, you know we have the test every Friday. You have the whole week to study."

If he had given us just one minute to memorize, I would have been okay, but he didn't. I got the worst grade I ever got in spelling. My grade was so bad, I'm not going to tell how many out of twenty I got. Or I should say how few.

We traded papers to grade them, and Tyrone always grabs mine and I do his. Tyrone started yelling, "Mr. Marshan! Mr. Marshan! I got a better grade than Marco! Hey, Mr. Marshan!"

That's how bad my grade was.

Lateesha said, "Tyrone got a better grade than Marco? Oh, Marco!"

And old skinny Miriam was giggling, and Robert, who I used to think was one of my friends, laughed at me. All of them.

I pretended like I didn't care. "Mr. Marshan, that was some jerky word list you gave us this week. Who needs nerdy words like those? You *know* I only study good words."

Mr. Marshan told everybody to quiet down, but Tyrone kept leaning over his desk toward me. "Marco, hey, Marco, Marco, what happened to you on the spelling test?"

I felt like I had a monster inside me. My monster made me twist around and pick up the edge of Tyrone's desk. I dumped it back in his lap, and all his papers and other stuff fell on the floor.

The weird thing was that nobody seemed to

know I did it. They all blamed it on Tyrone.

Mr. Marshan said, "Tyrone! What are you doing? I'm getting tired of all the commotion."

Now, nobody gets in Tyrone's face, ever. He didn't care who was getting blamed. All he cared about was, you don't do that to him. He kicked away the desk and came flying through the air at me. He was yelling curses and throwing punches. One got me right in the neck, and oh man, my head was turning around. I crawled under my desk to get away from him.

Robert and a bunch of them got hold of Tyrone. Mr. Marshan made him pick up his stuff and go sit in the back of the room in the Cool-Off Chair. Mr. Marshan told Tyrone he had better develop some self-control pronto or there was going to be a play with no Main Monster in it. "This is Strike One, Tyrone," he said. "You know the rule—Three Strikes and You're Out."

Tyrone shook his shoulders and stomped his feet and growled. But he never told the teacher that I started it. Even when he wants to beat you up, Tyrone won't betray you. Mr. Marshan asked me if I was okay, and the kids all looked at me, and everybody sat back down and turned their backs on Tyrone.

That was only the beginning of the bad afternoon.

At two forty-five, time to pack up and go home, I sneaked a look back at Tyrone. He wasn't in the Cool-Off Chair. I thought maybe he had gone into the coatroom to get his jacket. When I turned back around, I saw Mrs. Gates in the doorway. First Tyrone, and now it was going to be Ritzi again.

I was right. She told me to come with her. We started walking toward the office. "Marco," she said, "I'm going to tell you straight out. Mrs. Rettle has accused your sister of causing the death of a gerbil."

I stopped, but she kept walking, so I had to run to catch up. "Ritzi is not a killer, Mrs. Gates!"

"I understand. You don't believe your little sister did such a thing. I can't say I believe it either. But Mrs. Rettle says she has proof positive, not just the circumstance of your sister's disappearance."

"Ritzi disappeared?"

"She ran out of the building, but we already heard from your uncle. She went to his store."

I said, "If anybody killed a gerbil, it was Mrs. Rettle."

"It seems to me," said Mrs. Gates, lifting her eyebrow a certain way, "it seems to me that there are altogether too many accusations flying around this school today."

But I was thinking that Mrs. Rettle was a liar and a cheat and a stinking rotten potato, and suddenly there she was in front of the school-office door with her whole class of little kids—except for Ritzi. The kids were standing in the hall crying. And not just plain old crying, either; they were howling.

Mrs. Gates said, "Mrs. Rettle, why have you brought these children here? Children, don't mill around like lost lambs! Form lines! Form lines at once!"

And then I saw why the children were howling. Mrs. Rettle was holding a shoe box. She tipped it so we could see it better. In the box on some Kleenex was this little ball of fur with its guts out. I'm in the fourth grade, and I almost puked when I saw it, so no wonder those little kids were howling.

Mrs. Rettle started yelling at me. "Do you see? Do you see what she did?"

I sort of got behind Mrs. Gates and yelled, "My sister never killed your gerbil!"

"Mrs. Rettle," said Mrs. Gates. "*Why* have you brought the children here?"

"I was bringing the evidence. They just followed along."

"Please give me that thing and take your children back. Calm them down and dismiss them. No, on second thought, leave *that* in the office, and you and I both will take your children back and dismiss them."

"I'll leave it," said Mrs. Rettle, "but I don't want it destroyed. This is evidence! Don't leave it with that boy." She snatched the box up in the air like I was going to take it away from her. "He'll destroy the evidence!"

"Mrs. Rettle!" said Mrs. Gates. "This is a school, not a police station! And this is *my* school. Now give me the box."

Mrs. Rettle gave it to her. "Keep it away from *him*."

"I wouldn't touch it!" I said. "And my sister would never do such a thing!"

"All right, Marco," said Mrs. Gates. "That's enough."

They left me and the dead gerbil in the office and went back with the howling little children. Mrs. Allen, the secretary, came over and said, "Doesn't this box have a lid?" Then she picked up a newspaper and laid it over the box. "We don't have to look at that, do we, Marco?" she said.

I sat on a bench and waited and tried not to look at the box. Then I started thinking about last fall when Uncle Albert had his hernia operation. Ritzi was talking about operations all the time then. One day she rolled my dog Lucy over on her back and marked on her belly with Magic Marker.

I thought, Ritzi would never hurt a live animal. She knows a live animal from a Barbie.

But somehow that little gerbil ended up dead. That seemed the worst of all. Whatever had happened, the little gerbil was the one dead.

Mr. Marshan came in the office. He had his baseball hat on, ready to go home, and he was carrying some shopping bags full of science reports and also my backpack. "I went in the coatroom and got your backpack, Marco," he said. "I put your library book in it." Then he said, "What happened with your sister?"

"She didn't kill the gerbil."

He seemed to have something else on his mind. "I wanted to ask you. Did you see if any of the kids . . . did you see anyone borrow the Monster head? We put it back in the garbage bag, didn't we? And we put it back in the coatroom? I'm sure we did. It's not there now. I guess I should go back and look again."

But he kept standing there.

"I didn't borrow it, Mr. Marshan," I said.

"I know, I know." Finally he said, "Marco, did you see Tyrone? I'm not sure he was there when I dismissed the class."

It felt like too much to me. It felt like all kinds of things falling down on my head. "I don't know nothing about Tyrone," I said.

Mr. Marshan and I looked at each other, and I could see what he was thinking. I was thinking the same thing. I thought the Monster head was probably wherever Tyrone was.

"Well," said Mr. Marshan. "I guess I'll go back to the room and look one more time before I leave."

I said, "Mr. Marshan, if Tyrone took it—not that I think he did, but *if* he did—it would just be borrowing because he wanted to show his mother."

And then, I didn't mean to, but with all of that happening—Tyrone hitting me and the spelling test and the dead gerbil and Ritzi and the Monster head—I started to cry.

It was awful to start crying in the office, in front of Mr. Marshan and Mrs. Allen and the children waiting for detention. Mrs. Gates came back and took me and Mr. Marshan into her office. Mr. Marshan put his hand on my shoulder and told me about how It's Good for Men to Cry. But I wasn't doing it because I wanted to. I was doing it because all this bad stuff had poured down through my head and was coming out my eyeballs. I blew my nose and looked at the pictures of Mrs. Gates's children on her desk. The girl was in a graduation gown and the boy was in a Marines uniform.

Mrs. Gates pulled out Ritzi's emergency card and called my mother at work. I could hear my mother yelling through the phone, she was so mad at Mrs. Rettle.

Hearing Mama yell made me feel a lot better. She wasn't going to let anything bad happen to Ritzi.

"I hear what you're saying," Mrs. Gates said to Mama.

Mrs. Gates said everyone had the weekend to think things over, and they would have a big meeting first thing Monday morning and straighten it all out.

She hung up the phone carefully. Then she looked at Mr. Marshan. "We'll put the corpse in a plastic bag in the refrigerator," she said. "Mrs. Rettle doesn't want to take a chance on it being thrown away."

"I'll do it," said Mr. Marshan. "But it had

better go in the freezer." He asked me if I'd be okay, and then he left.

Mrs. Gates took a long look at the photographs of her children. "Yes," she said, "we'll work it out by Monday, one way or the other. Now, Marco. You are to go to your uncle's store and pick up Ritzi. You and your sister and your mother should have a nice, relaxing weekend. Do your homework early, that's what I always told my children. Get it out of the way. On Monday we'll clear all this up."

I started off for home feeling like the biggest problem was Tyrone borrowing the head to show his mother and probably getting Strike Two. I thought that was the biggest problem, but the bad afternoon was not over yet.

4

A BAD
AFTERNOON
GETS WORSE

Uncle Albert's friend Big Frank was sitting in the store on a chair. Big Frank was watching the news channel, and Uncle Albert was reading the horse-racing newspaper. Big Frank just about fills up the whole store, except for the back room where Uncle Albert's guard dog, Brown-o, lives.

Uncle Albert said, "Now here comes the other one. Are you in trouble too? How can a girl the size of your sister get in trouble? You want something to eat? They're always hungry, these kids."

I started to say no, but he had already put down his paper and started making me a milk-coffee. He puts in a lot of hot milk and a lot of sugar and a little bit of coffee.

I said. "Hey, Uncle Albert, where is she?"

"The baby-sitter with the bird came by and Ritzi went home with her. You and your sister eat up all my profits, you know that, don't you?"

"Leave the kid alone, Al," said Big Frank.

"He's my nephew," said Uncle Albert. "He knows what I mean. Him and the little girl, they eat like football players. *She* asked not only for a roll and butter to eat, but two rolls and butter to go, do you believe that? That lady with the bird said she'd give her a snack, but no, the little girl wants to take home two rolls in a bag. I'm telling you. They eat you out of house and store."

But all the time he was buttering up a roll for me. That's the way my Uncle Albert is. You have to listen to what he does, not to what he says.

I drank my milk-coffee, and after a while I said, "Uncle Albert, have you seen Tyrone?"

"No. But if you see him, you tell him to get over here and sweep my floor. He's supposed to work for me."

I went down the hill to our building eating my roll and butter. I looked for Tyrone everywhere as I went. I passed the hubcap man. He collects them when they pop off of cars down on the avenue. After his store comes the building with Sister Serena's Fortune-Telling. My mother says you should never trust your fortune to someone who lives in her store and cooks on a hot plate. Next comes our building, which is the best one on the block, if I may say so myself.

Instead of stopping at our apartment, I went straight to the parrot lady's. I could hear her television, and I could hear her bird squawk. She opened the door just a little crack. About all I could see was one eye. She said, "Your little sister took the key and went downstairs. Tell your mother I kept her half an hour." Then she closed the door.

I thought I heard a dog bark. I thought maybe it was my little dog Lucy, but it sounded too far away. As soon as I got to our floor, I saw something funny.

Ritzi's key was in the lock. It looked like the key got stuck and someone just left it there. When I touched the door, it swung open.

"Ritzi?" I called, and my voice made a little echo.

It is a very scary thing to go in your house when it is totally silent in there: no dog, no sister. "Ritzi?" I said. "Here, Lucy, here girl." Ritzi might hide, but my little dog would always come. They were not there.

Neither were the Barbies. That scared me even more. There was not a Barbie in the house. She took the Barbies, and she took her two rolls with butter, and she took Lucy's leash, and she took Lucy.

"Ritzi," I said out loud, as if she could hear me, "you can run away if you want to, but you got no right to take my dog!"

Then I talked to myself. You're a smart kid, Marco, I said. Sometimes you even see things other people don't see. So squeeze your eyes shut, and see where your sister is.

I squeezed my eyes shut. I saw only black, and I heard my heart beating.

I opened my eyes and tried to use my brain like a detective in a mystery. I had heard a dog bark. Did that mean Ritzi ran out while I was upstairs at the parrot lady's?

I started to go out. Halfway downstairs, I remembered I left the door open, so I had to go back and lock the door. I got outside and looked up and down the street. I had to choose a direction. Down the hill are the abandoned buildings where the druggies hang out. At the very bottom of the hill is an empty lot with a lot of cartons and pieces of cars and stoves and a house made out of cardboard, where Crazy Wee-wee lives.

Crazy Wee-wee is about the scariest person on our block. You can't tell where his hair ends and his beard and his mustache start, and his eyes are two different colors. Also, he keeps his hands out in front of him and never lets his fingers touch each other. He talks to himself, and once he captured my dog Lucy, but I got her back. Ever since then, Lucy doesn't like to go down the hill. She always wants to go up the hill to the park.

I chose up.

Sister Serena was sitting in front of her big window with a bowl full of meat. I knocked on the door and went in. "Good afternoon, Sister Serena, have you seen my little sister? She's small and wears tights, and she had a dog with her."

"Yes," she said. She gazed at me. Her eyes always make me nervous. "I saw her."

"Did she go *up* the hill, Sister Serena?"

Sister Serena raised one hand with meat loaf all over it, and I thought she was going to point, but she just scratched her nose. "Maybe," she said. "I don't know."

"Okay," I said, backing out. "Thank you! Thank you very much!"

The hubcap man was nailing up another hubcap on his wall. Uncle Albert once tried to buy one from him, but he said it was a collector's item. "Excuse me," I said, "do you know my little sister? Did she come by this way? She had a dog with her."

"The little girl with the little dog? They went up the hill."

"Just now?"

He rubbed his chin. "Yeah. Just now."

I felt much better. I was on the trail. I would catch up to her, and oh man, was I going to give it to Ritzi because of all this trouble! This running-away stuff has to stop, Ritzi, I was going to say.

When I got to the stoplight, I saw Tyrone on the other corner. He was wearing his Bad Dude look. He acted like he didn't see me, but I crossed over anyhow. At least he didn't have the Monster head.

"Hey, Tyrone!" I said.

He sucked his teeth and looked over my head like I was some pigeon pecking at the street garbage.

"Tyrone," I said, "Ritzi ran away again."

"So?" said Tyrone.

"Mrs. Rettle said she murdered a gerbil. Do you believe that?" I didn't like the way he was acting. He was cold and mean. I said, "So did you see Ritzi, Tyrone?"

"Why would I be looking for your little sister, Marco?"

"I didn't say were you *looking*, I just said, did you see her pass by?"

He filled up his mouth with a big spit, and he shot it out on one side of me.

He said, "If your little sister is missing, Marco, why don't you use some of your magic powers and look through buildings for her?"

Now, I never claimed to be able to see through buildings. It is just that sometimes I can do certain things, and sometimes I can see certain things.

I said, "I still have my powers, Tyrone. My powers are always with me."

"Yeah, right. You and Superman." He was insulting me, but at least he was talking. He was more like himself.

I said, "My powers only come when they want to."

"Yeah, right," said Tyrone.

"Well, I'm going to the park to find my sister now."

"So go."

Of course I wanted him to come with me. With two of us we could find her in no time.

"So I'm going," I said.

Tyrone just stood there with his hands in the pockets of his pants, looking away from me.

I thought, His mother doesn't even buy him a good coat. Every winter my mother buys me a new down jacket. Tyrone wears raggedy old clothes.

But I didn't say it out loud. I walked slowly up the hill by myself.

I had never been in the park alone. I had been up there with my dog, with my sister, and with my mother. Tyrone and I go up there all the time, but I never was there by myself all alone. No cars were allowed on Park Drive, so the joggers and the bicyclers and the people with baby carriages can go along on the smooth road. But I saw only one jogger that day.

I wished for Tyrone. It was getting cold, too, and I started thinking Ritzi was going to freeze if she stayed out here alone. She is small for her age and skinny.

I saw some boys I didn't know sitting on some benches, so I decided to go in the other direction. Those boys looked like they were from the Other Side of the Park. One of them was tall with a long black leather coat. One was fat with cutoff jeans and no coat. One was about my size, and he looked like he was bald-headed.

Mama says, over there, on the Other Side of the Park, you need more than a spirit guardian. She says you need a bodyguard with a machine gun.

I walked fast toward the baby playground. There is a better playground with wooden ships and castles farther on, but the baby playground was nearest. It just has a couple of swings and one big flying-saucer thing like an upside-down bowl with holes you can climb through. I stood for a minute looking at the empty playground. Then I turned around and—

Here came the boys from the Other Side of the Park.

There was nobody behind me in the baby park. On Park Drive there was not a bicycle, not a jogger, not even a baby-sitter with a stroller.

And these ugly boys were coming after me.

The one with the black leather coat pointed, and they spread out and started to come faster.

Maybe I could have been cool and walked on like I owned the place. Maybe if I hadn't been alone. But I was by myself, so I started to run.

I could hear the wind in my ears and I could hear feet running behind me. I could see the wall to the street, and I meant to jump out of the park. I thought I would make it okay.

But the small boy with the bald head was a very fast kid. He caught up to me, and he cut me off!

I ran into the baby playground. The fat boy was already there. I was surrounded.

They stopped running and came at me slowly. Tyrone would have just tackled one of them and started fighting. But Tyrone likes to fight. I always think about getting hurt. I think about hits in my ribs and knives and kicks Where It Really Hurts.

I bumped into the upside-down saucer thing. Real quick I turned around and climbed to the top of it. I said to myself, Marco, you are not much of a fighter, so do something smart.

I pretended I knew karate. All I really know about karate is what I see in the movies, and what Robert in my class shows us. He takes karate and has a belt; I forget what color. I put one leg behind me and I stuck my hands up like sharp knives. "Hiya!" I yelled. "Watch out, jerk-heads, I wear a black belt when I'm in a *good* mood!"

My idea was to stop them for one second, and then drop through a hole in the saucer thing and run between them. It wasn't much of an idea, but they stopped.

Suddenly we heard this weird sound behind us: *Sssssssh! Sssssssh!*

Then we heard some kind of howling. We all looked toward Park Drive. The biggest stick I ever saw was whirling around and around— whirling around Tyrone! He was swinging it around so fast it went *Sssssssh!* He was howling. He started picking up speed and running down the hill. I never saw anybody look so good in my whole life!

I jumped up and down and yelled, "Here comes Big Foot of the Jungle! You are dead now! That's Wild Man Tyrone! He eats kids for junk food!"

They stood there staring.

"Run for your lives!" I yelled.

While they were deciding whether to run or fight, I dropped through the nearest hole. The bald-headed boy saw me, and *whop!* He hit me in the back, but it wasn't a good hit. The next thing I knew, Tyrone had knocked him in the side with the big stick. Tyrone circled around and around with the stick, yelling, "Merry-go-round!"

The boys were cursing and running in different directions. I dodged the fat boy and ran to the swings. "Come on, Tyrone," I said, and I pushed a swing at the fat boy.

Tyrone had gone wild. "I'm going to mess me up one of these banana brains! Whoo—ooo—ow!"

Well, the bad guys finally figured out that

Tyrone was just a kid too, so they picked up rocks and sticks and threw them at us. One rock hit me right on the side of my head. For a second I thought I was going to faint, but I didn't. I just threw the rocks back at them.

I don't know what would have happened, except that some little children from an after-school program came over the hill. There was a whole bunch of them, all these little pink, blue, and yellow caps and coats. The teacher started yelling at us. I think she was yelling at Tyrone, but it didn't matter, because the boys from the Other Side decided they had had enough.

Tyrone wanted to go after them, but I grabbed his arm and slowed him down. He looked at me sideways and grinned like his old self. "I scared those nerditos pretty bad, didn't I, Marco? Yeah, I'm the Wild Man of the Jungle all right. Who needs magic, right, Marco? You're pretty lucky I trailed you up here."

"Tyrone," I said, "I'll tell you the truth. I am *very* lucky you trailed me up here. You're the best friend I ever had. You saved me from these guys, and you never turned me in to

Mr. Marshan today. You're all right, Tyrone."

He always puts his head down when somebody says something nice to him.

I said, "We're blood brothers, Tyrone. We stand together! Right? You stand for me, and I stand for you!"

He looked up and gave me his biggest grin. "Always," he said.

And I said, "Always."

"So Marco," he said. "What are we waiting for? Let's go find your little sister."

5
DEAD DOLLS

Tyrone and I went looking for Ritzi. I told him all the details about the dead gerbil. "And then, on top of everything," I said, "Mr. Marshan said the Monster head is missing. For a minute I thought *you* took it, Tyrone."

Tyrone swung his big stick around and smashed some bushes with it. He said, "Mr. Marshan was dismissing the kids. I was in the back of the room by myself. Nobody was looking."

"You *took* it, Tyrone?"

"I borrowed it. To show to my mother, that's all." He swung his stick around his head again and then let it loose. It went flying off into the woods. "She don't believe I'm the Main Monster."

"Oh man, Tyrone! Oh man! That's Two Strikes! Two Strikes against you!"

"I put it in a safe place," he said. "She wasn't home, so I put it in a safe place."

"You didn't put it at your house, did you?"

"What do you think, I'm stupid? Those people over there would sell it before it touched the floor. I put it in the Dumpster."

I couldn't believe it. "You mean the *garbage* Dumpster? Behind the school, where the cats live? Somebody will think it's garbage!"

"That's why nobody will steal it. They'll think it's garbage."

"Somebody could come and drop more garbage on it and smash it up! They could collect the garbage and cart it away!"

"They don't collect garbage at night. Nobody will look for it there. It's a good place. Where would you put it?"

"I wouldn't take it in the first place! Now *you're* in trouble and my *sister* is in trouble. I can't believe this!"

Tyrone gave me a look. "Oh, Marco the angel," he said. "Marco the big-shot super-power angel. You ran off after your sister and never even told anyone."

"That's because I was going to find her and get her back before anyone knew!"

"So I was going to take back the head before Mr. Marshan knew."

"But you didn't!"

"So I have bad luck, okay, Marco? I am a Bad Luck Kid, and you are a Good Luck Kid. Does that make you happy?"

Actually, at that moment I was feeling like everybody's luck was running bad. It was getting colder and windier, and my jacket didn't cover my legs, and my ears were getting cold too.

Just the same, I was glad Tyrone was walking with me. I said, "Are you going to help me find Ritzi? I need to know."

He looked like I had hurt his feelings.

"What do you think, Marco? Sure I'm going to help you find her."

Ritzi wasn't at the big playground, so we walked over to the playing fields. Some kids were trying to fly kites in the wind. The kites kept crashing. There was also a man with two of the biggest dogs I ever saw. We took a long-cut around him.

The playing fields are in the middle of the park. They divide our side from the Other Side. At the end of the playing fields there are hills and trees, and it gets much darker.

We came to a lake full of brown leaves. I had never been this far before. A couple of seagulls were walking around poking at candy wrappers.

"I don't know, Marco," said Tyrone. "It's a big park."

I knew Tyrone wouldn't give up, but I was afraid anyhow. I said, "Let's try calling Lucy. She didn't run away; she just went because Ritzi took her."

So we faced in opposite directions and yelled, "Lucy! Lucy! Here, girl!" I gave my special whistle, but nothing happened except one of the seagulls flapped its wings.

We started to walk again. I said, "Tyrone, you've been here before, haven't you?"

"Not right here at this exact place."

"Tyrone, we're almost to the Other Side!"

He said, "What do you want me to do about it? Do you want to go back? Maybe Ritzi got hungry and went home."

"I don't think so," I said. "I think she's afraid they're going to put her in jail or something."

"For killing a *gerbil*?"

"I didn't say *I* think she's going to jail. She took her Barbies and she borrowed Lucy and she got rolls and butter from Uncle Albert. I don't think she's coming home."

"Well," said Tyrone, "that's stupid. Nobody does anything bad to little kids. Little kids have it easy. If a kid my size gets in trouble, they send him to Juvenile."

The path made more twists and turns. My feet felt slow and heavy. They seemed to want to go back. More and more of me wanted to go back. There was a little voice in my brain trying to make my mouth say *Tyrone, let's go home.*

Then I had a Mental Sight. Just a little one. Suddenly I could see Ritzi. I couldn't see where she was, only that she was in a dark place. She was so quiet that I could tell she was the most scared she had ever been in her whole life.

In my mind I said, Ritzi, you dope, why did you run away? Why didn't you tell me or Mama or Uncle Albert or somebody? What can you do on your own without any help? I was so busy thinking these thoughts that I bumped into Tyrone and almost pushed him into—

A man.

"Look out!" yelled Tyrone. He jumped off to the side.

But I froze. I was face-to-face with Crazy Wee-wee.

Yes, Crazy Wee-wee who lives in a box at the bottom of the hill and scares children. His gray eye followed after Tyrone, and his blue eye was on me.

Crazy Wee-wee seemed like he was frozen too. Tyrone was yelling for me. I was staring at

Crazy Wee-wee's blue eye. He opened and shut his mouth a few times and made a croaking sound. I took some steps backward, and I heard Tyrone say, "Talk to him, Marco."

He didn't look quite as mean as when he protects his little cardboard house. So I said, "Hey, Mr. Crazy Wee-wee. How are you? I never knew you came up to this park. You come up to this park often? We're up here looking for my little sister and my dog. You know my little dog, don't you? You know me, I'm Marco, I live in three-eleven, on your same block. And this is Tyrone, he lives down your way—"

One of Crazy Wee-wee's hands sort of went over his shoulder, like he was throwing something or maybe pointing.

Then the other hand moved crossways under his chin like he was cutting his throat.

Then I understood what he was saying. "Dolls." He pointed behind him. "Dead dolls."

It went through me like someone poured ice water through my guts. I didn't know what it meant, but it sounded very bad for Ritzi.

"Hey, Marco," said Tyrone. "He's talking about your sister's dolls."

We couldn't just sneak away sideways. We had to go where he had been. We had to go around Crazy Wee-wee and see what he had seen. We made a big circle off the path and through the bushes. He kept trying to tell us not to go on, but we did.

"Oh man, Tyrone," I said. "This is bad. This is very bad."

"Ah, he's crazy," said Tyrone, but I could tell by his voice that Tyrone thought it was bad too.

"Maybe we shouldn't stay on the path," I said. We were coming to a big curve. You couldn't see what came next.

I turned around to check that Crazy Wee-wee wasn't following us. I was as bad as my dog Lucy, turning in circles, walking sideways, then backward.

Suddenly Tyrone yelled, and I did too! Something jumped in my face and on my shoulders! On my shoulders, on my back, little people with no arms!

"The dolls!" I screamed. "Ritzi's dolls!"

Both of us were caught in a spiderweb of bald-headed Barbies tied across the path. A whole string of them, with their arms off and sticks through their armholes, hanging across the path, on Lucy's leash.

"Look at this," said Tyrone. He had found a piece of paper. He held it up and read, " 'Bwar.' What's 'Bwar'?"

"Let me see," I said. Written on the paper in purple crayon was BWAR and DANGR. "It's 'Beware' and 'Danger,' " I said. "That's Ritzi's writing. Ritzi put these dolls up here."

"That's not how you spell *danger*," Tyrone said. "I thought Ritzi was supposed to be smart."

"She's in kindergarten, Tyrone," I said. "Most of the kids can't even make a *D*."

In front of us was a circle of benches almost hidden in the trees. There were broken whiskey bottles and worse lying around there.

"Call the dog," said Tyrone.

"Lucy!" I shouted. "Lucy! Come here, girl! Here, Lucy!"

We heard a bark!

It was the happiest sound I ever heard. A little bark, and then a scrabbling noise, and here came Lucy—*zoom!*—through the air and—*whomp!*—right up into my arms. She started licking me and wiggling, and I knew everything was going to be okay.

"All right!" said Tyrone. "We found the dolls, and we found the dog, so where's your sister?"

"Lucy," I said, "find Ritzi."

Like a trained dog actor, Lucy went *yip! yip!* and jumped down and ran under a bench toward a little shed on the other side of the benches. This shed had a lot of electrical wires coming out of it. Tyrone looked at me, and I looked at Tyrone, and we followed Lucy.

The metal door had a lock, but one corner of the door was bent out. Lucy stood there barking. I squatted and looked in.

It was just like my Mental Sight. Ritzi was in a little human mouse nest under a lot of wires and fuses. She was hugging her WELCOME TO PUERTO RICO bag, and she didn't move.

I said, "Ritzi, man, we looked everywhere for you!"

She was so scared, I had to pull her out, and right away she grabbed my waist and hugged me so hard I almost fell over. She smelled like dirt.

Tyrone squatted down and hopped at the same time. "Hey, Ritzi!" he said. "Come on, Little Ritz, don't cry, Ritzi! You knew me and Marco, we'd find you. Hey! You our main little girl. You part of the posse, Little Ritz!"

She said something I couldn't hear because her face was in my coat. I made her stand out a little bit. She said, "Marco, don't let them take me to Foster Care!"

"Who said that?" I said. "Who told you they were going to take you to Foster Care? Did Mrs. Rettle say that? You know Mama wouldn't let them. Who said that?"

"Because of the gerbil, but I didn't do it, Marco! I didn't do anything to the gerbil."

Tyrone said, "You don't get sent to Foster Care or Juvenile for messing with animals. I should know, because of all those mangy old cats that used to live in my basement."

Ritzi stopped crying and looked interested. "What did you do to the cats?"

"Nothing," said Tyrone. "I used to play with them. You know, tied stuff to their tails, put them in boxes."

Ritzi said, "You shouldn't do that, Tyrone! You should think of how the cats feel."

"I know how they feel. They feel mad. One of them scratched me in the face."

"Let's go home," I said. "Maybe we can get home before anybody starts to worry about us."

"I wasn't never going to go home," said Ritzi, and her face looked almost like she might cry again.

"Hey, Ritzi," said Tyrone. "You know what? You know what I got today? I got the Main Monster head. Wait till you see the Main Monster head! Oh man, is it bad! Awesome! I'm going to take you to see the Monster head!"

But first we had to unstring all the Barbies and put them in the straw bag. And then Lucy wanted to play and wouldn't go back on the leash, so we had to chase her.

"You should train your dog better, Marco," said Tyrone. "And your little sister."

When we finally caught Lucy and got her back on the leash, it was almost dark. But we thought everything was okay, because we were near the park exit.

6
THE OTHER SIDE OF THE PARK

There was just one problem. We were on the wrong side of the park. When you come out on our side, you see big houses and trees and doctor offices and a school for rich kids. But over here there were no trees, and the buildings had fire escapes in front. One house had sheets of metal over all the windows.

"Tyrone," I whispered. "We shouldn't be here, Tyrone. This is the Other Side of the Park!"

"I have to go to the bathroom," said Ritzi.

Tyrone said, "I guess we could go back the way we came."

I looked back. The trees were dark and tight together. I looked down the street with no trees at all. Some men were standing around a big can with a fire in it. Past them was something that was maybe a phone booth.

I said, "Let's call Uncle Albert. Or maybe Mama is home. She'll come and get us in a taxi."

"You think so?" said Tyrone. "In a taxi?"

"Sure, why not," I said, but all the time I was thinking those men with the fire looked like the guys who hang out on our block, only older and meaner.

Ritzi was starting to jiggle up and down.

"Let's go find a phone," said Tyrone.

We started to walk, and then I remembered. I had left without one penny. I put my hand way down in my jacket and found nothing. I said, "Hey, Tyrone, I don't have any money."

Tyrone felt around in all his pockets and didn't find anything either.

"You should have money!" I said. "You have a job!"

"Me! Why don't *you* have money? What are you yelling at me for?"

Ritzi said, "I brought my money." She stopped jiggling and put down her bag. She had to lay out all the Barbies on the sidewalk. At the very bottom of her bag was a little clear plastic pocketbook. You could see the money inside, quarters and dimes and a dollar. She handed the pocketbook to me.

"That's good," said Tyrone. "Little Ritz has the money."

Then we had to wait for her to shove the Barbies back in the bag. We tried to help her, but she said we were hurting them.

We still had to pass the men with the fire. We slowed down, and Tyrone put on his Bad Dude face. I picked up my dog to carry her. She growled at the men's backs, but they did not even look at us. They were just laughing and talking and having themselves a little party.

When we got past the men with the fire, I saw a store across the street. I was thinking that maybe we could go over there. I was thinking that maybe there would be a man like Uncle Albert who talked grouchy but was nice inside. I saw a lady down at the corner too, getting ready to cross the street. She looked like a grandmother, and I thought, Well, maybe they have uncles and grandmothers on the Other Side of the Park too.

Then Tyrone stopped. I turned around.

It was your Worst Nightmare. Climbing over the wall from the park were the three ugly boys from the playground: the fat one with bare legs, the one with the leather coat, and the little bald-headed kid who could outrun me.

Ritzi and I had been in front, and I was still carrying Lucy and the pocketbook. When we turned around, Tyrone was between us and the Ugly Crew. I could see Tyrone's back, and I could see their fronts. The one in the leather coat sucked his teeth. The fat one hitched up his pants. The little mean one made a fist and smacked it into his other hand.

Tyrone said, "Lookahere, it's Nerdito and the Banana Brain Crew." He made a motion with his hand, like Come on, Marco, let's take these suckers out.

There were only three of them, and my little dog Lucy was already growling. *She* has a lot of heart when it comes to fighting. We had a good chance, especially with a fighter like Tyrone. We would have had a good chance to fight them and win.

But something happened inside me. My feet started backing up. I had Lucy and Ritzi, and inside me was a little squealing coward monster.

I didn't even say good-bye to Tyrone. He didn't know I was running out on him. He thought his so-called friend Marco was backing him up.

I, Marco, who said I would always stand by my man Tyrone, ran away. I left him to face the Ugly Crew alone! I ran, bouncing Lucy in my arms and dragging Ritzi. Ritzi was yelling something and pulling back, and Lucy went *yip yip yip*, but I wouldn't stop for nothing. I was full of the wind of fear. The little coward inside me was squealing, and all I could think was to get away. To get to the phone booth and the grandmother lady waiting for the light to change.

I didn't look back. I didn't let go of Ritzi until I reached for the phone—

But there was no phone. Someone had torn it off, and just a wire was hanging there. Lucy was still trying to get loose and go fight, and Ritzi started to go back too. She said, "Marco, I have to—"

"You don't have to anything!" I said, and grabbed her. Finally I looked back.

It was the weirdest thing. They were gone. Like magic. Disappeared! Tyrone was gone, and the Ugly Crew was gone. The men were still laughing around their fire, but no Ugly Crew, no Tyrone.

"Let me go!" said Ritzi. "Let me go!"

Yip yip, said Lucy.

The grandmother lady was looking at us funny. "She's my sister," I said. "I'm not kidnapping her. She has to go to the bathroom."

Ritzi yelled, "Marco, I lost No-Arm No-Leg! You and Tyrone made me leave her!"

"Are you crazy?" I said. "We aren't going back for a doll. Forget it, Ritzi, no way!"

She stomped her foot. "I have to I have to!" she said. "That was No-Arm No-Leg! I can't leave her."

At that moment the light changed, and a police car pulled up to the corner. Ritzi was screaming and Lucy was barking and jumping, but I dragged them both right out into the street. The police rolled down their window.

"I'm not kidnapping her!" I said to the police.

Ritzi yelled, "I want No-Arm!"

"Who?" said the police officer. He looked pretty nice, which made me want to cry.

"We got lost in the park," I said. "We don't know how to get back. And my sister has to go to the bathroom real bad and Tyrone disappeared." I took a deep breath. "Tyrone was being attacked by some bad guys."

"So was No-Arm No-Leg!" said Ritzi.

"Hop in," said the cop.

We got to sit in the back, in the cage for

Perpetrators, and I felt like that's where I belonged—in a cage—because of how I ran out on Tyrone.

They wanted to know our address, and where we came out of the park. I pointed and said, "Right there, that's where we came out, and that's where I lost my friend." I said "lost," but I should have said "betrayed."

"That's where I dropped No-Arm!" said Ritzi. The police slowed down the car, but there was nothing on the sidewalk.

"You see," I said. "She isn't there, Ritzi. She's in the bottom of your bag."

"She's gone," Ritzi said. "She'll be eaten by rats."

They drove us around inside the park. We looked right and left, but it seemed like Tyrone and those guys had fought each other till there was not a scrap left of any of them.

Ritzi whispered, "Marco, I have to go to the bathroom *bad*."

The policeman must have heard her, because he said, "Five minutes and you'll be home."

I started to see familiar things: the bikers

and joggers and the big playground and then the baby playground where Tyrone had saved me. We came out on the street with the mansions, and started down the hill.

The policeman said, "I expect your friend went home a different way. But we'll keep an eye out for him."

I felt sick to my stomach. I was going along with them, even though I knew Tyrone was still in trouble. I was still betraying Tyrone.

Then I saw Mama walking up the street. She was walking fast, and it looked like she was going toward Uncle Albert's store. I said, "Stop the car! That's our mother!"

Boy, was she surprised! She had come home early, and she didn't even know yet that we were missing. She thought we were at Uncle Albert's store, and Uncle Albert and the parrot lady both thought we were somewhere else. Mama hugged us, and Lucy jumped all over, and Ritzi started telling about how No-Arm No-Leg had been eaten by rats, and the police explained, and I explained, and it looked like a happy ending.

But inside I was thinking: *Tyrone Tyrone Tyrone.*

On the way home, Mama yelled at us a little bit. She said we were going to turn her hair gray and how is a single mother supposed to do her job when her kids keep running off and not telling her where they're going.

But she looked a lot happier than either me or Ritzi. Ritzi sat on the couch and laid out her Barbies one by one, and she was right, there was no No-Arm.

But she just lost half a doll. I lost Tyrone.

Mama said, "What do you kids want for dinner? Marco, you should choose. Do you want spaghetti? Do you want me to cook the chicken in the refrigerator? You choose, because you saved Ritzi. Then I'll go out and get ice cream after dinner."

I said, "Mama, you are treating me like I did something good, but I did something bad. I left Tyrone there. I betrayed my best friend."

"You're in the fourth grade, Marco. You're too young to betray someone." She got down the big pot. "We'll have spaghetti. That's your favorite, right, Marco?"

"You don't understand," I said. "Tyrone was holding off these bad guys. He thought I was backing him up. He maybe gave his life for us!"

"Don't make a big soap opera out of this, Marco! You had to take care of Ritzi. Tyrone knows how to take care of himself. He is From the Streets."

I know what she means about Tyrone, that he is From the Streets, but he never wanted to be. It was just his luck.

After dinner, Mama said she was going to go to Uncle Albert's to get us some ice cream.

"I'll go," I said. "I can run up there real quick."

She gave me a look. "I don't want to hear you went to the park looking for Tyrone."

I promised her I wouldn't go to the park, not after dark, not a chance! Not me. "I'm too much a coward," I said.

I took Lucy with me, and she thought we were going up the hill to Uncle Albert's too, but I turned down the hill instead. I went to

Tyrone's building. I pushed the buzzer, which doesn't work very often. Then I banged on the door and yelled up to the second floor.

A window opened. It was Tyrone's mother. She has little tiny braids that stick out from her head, not the fancy ones with beads, just the kind to keep the hair out of your face.

"Who is that?" she yelled. "Tyrone?"

"It's Marco. Is Tyrone up there?"

"Why would I be yelling 'Is that Tyrone' if Tyrone was up here? That boy is never where he should be if anyone needs him. If you see him, you tell him to get his tail over here. I need him to get me some stuff."

I wondered how she would act if she knew her son Tyrone maybe gave his life for his friends. I said, "Tyrone got the best part in the school play."

"He said something about it, yeah."

"You should see him! You should see his Monster head."

"How come he has to be a monster?"

"It's the best part," I said. "Everybody wanted to be the Monster."

She made a noise like a grunt. "Well, you send him over here if you see him."

I started up the hill, but I didn't go to Uncle Albert's store. I didn't go to the park, either. I had a plan. I decided that even though I was a coward, I was going to do something for Tyrone.

7

THE TRUE PERPETRATOR

My idea was to get the head of the Monster out of the garbage Dumpster and pretend I was the one who took it.

If somebody said, "Marco, you are not the kind of boy who takes something without asking," I would answer, "I am like my friend Tyrone. We are both From the Streets."

I took the shortcut across the ball courts. I tried to use my powers to see what was ahead of me. There was nothing but long, tall shadows. Lucy didn't bark, so I said to myself:

This is not a Mental Sight, Marco, this is your imagination. Pay attention to your dog. If she don't care, you don't care. If a person is From the Streets, they can't jump at shadows.

So I was a little braver, because my little dog is brave. But I could still feel the coward in my heart.

When we got to the school, I made Lucy hold still. We listened to be sure nobody was following us. Then we sneaked along the back of the building.

When we got to the Dumpster, Lucy started to growl. It was her deep-in-the-throat growl that means there might be trouble ahead. I squinted my eyes. Something was moving around on the Dumpster. There was a little scrappy sound, and then it jumped off the Dumpster.

"It's a cat, Lucy," I said. "Just a cat."

She growled down in her throat again, but she always growls at cats.

Another cat appeared on top of the garbage. It sat on the rim and cleaned itself. "You see?" I said. "More cats."

Then I heard a different sound, and I stopped again. I got a better hold on the leash.

Something much bigger than a cat was coming around the Dumpster. Something with arms and legs and a big lump on one side. It was coming straight at us!

"Attack!" I screamed. "Attack, Lucy! Attack!"

I let go of the leash and Lucy ran at it. She leaped! But she wasn't biting; she was yipping with happiness. And the big thing put down its lump and laughed and picked her up.

I said, "Tyrone? Is that you, Tyrone?"

"Yeah, it's me. Where did you go, Marco? I looked everywhere for you."

"Tyrone!" I shouted. He was alive! I felt like jumping in his arms just like Lucy did. It was too dark to see his face, but he didn't *sound* mad. "We looked everywhere for you! We were in a police car."

"Oh yeah? I saw a police car, but I hid."

"You hid, Tyrone? We were in that police car trying to save you."

"Save me from what?

"From the Ugly Crew!"

He put Lucy down. "Ah, those guys. Those guys are punks. They can't even fight good. Three of them isn't enough to fight me! Do you know what I did, Marco? I turned myself into the Main Monster. Just like when we're rehearsing. I can scare anybody when I'm the Main Monster. I chased them into the park. They threw some stuff at me, but then they ran away when they saw the police car."

"I wish I had been there," I said. Then I remembered I *had* been there. "I had a monster in me too, Tyrone. Mine was this ugly little coward monster. I ran out on you, Tyrone."

"You're no good at fighting, Marco," he said. "Besides, you had to take care of Ritzi."

I felt bad because Tyrone thought I wasn't a fighter. I said, "I didn't stand behind you—"

"Oh, shut up, Marco, we did it like a team. I held them off and you went for help. That's the way it's s'posed to be." He bent down and picked up the lump. It was a garbage bag.

"Is that the head, Tyrone?"

"Yeah, and it never got touched by anything, not even a cat."

When he moved to show me the bag, light from the streetlight fell on his face.

"What happened to your face?"

"A little cut," he said. "One of the punks hit me with a rock."

I was just leaning over to get a better look at the cut when the cat that had been sitting on top of the Dumpster jumped down. It was Big Boss. Big Boss has a rip out of each ear and one eye was swollen shut. He walked by as close as he could, and Lucy went hoarse barking at him.

"That cat is disrespectful to my dog," I said.

Big Boss jumped down to the window and squeezed his fat, ugly self through the window into Ritzi's classroom.

"Look at that," said Tyrone. "That's the window to the kindergarten."

Even though it was the weekend and cold, the window was open. There was just enough light from the street to see Big Boss drop to the floor of the classroom. And there, near the window, were two big bowls of cat food, one wet and one dry, plus a bowl of water.

Tyrone said, "Big Boss cat walking in like he owned the place. He thinks this is Mickey D. McDonald's hamburger heaven."

Big Boss didn't even stand up to eat. He ate sitting on his fat tail. Lucy about strangled herself on the leash trying to get him.

Suddenly I had a Mental Sight of Mrs. Rettle. I saw the cat hairs on her skirt, and I saw her putting out the cat food. I saw it as clearly as if she were doing it right there, right then.

"Tyrone," I said, "Rotten Rettle leaves the window open. Rotten Rettle leaves food out for the cats!"

"So? My mother puts stuff on the fire escape for the cats too."

"But Tyrone, this is the *school*. This is the kindergarten where the gerbil got killed. Do you think Big Boss knows a mouse from a gerbil? Big Boss must have killed the gerbil! Rotten Rettle puts food out for the cats. She leaves the window open and lets the cats in, and then she blames my sister when a gerbil gets killed!"

"Aha," said Tyrone in a deep voice like a professional actor. "The mystery is solved."

"Yes, Tyrone," I said, "I think we have discovered the True Perpetrator." I could see us, Tyrone and me and Ritzi too, standing on blocks like at the Olympics, getting medals while the National Anthem played.

Tyrone put the bag with the Monster head over his shoulder like Santa Claus. "They won't believe us. It's kids' word against teacher's."

We went home as fast as we could, but just the same, Mama started to yell when we walked in the door. "Where's the ice cream? You didn't get the ice cream! You didn't go to Albert's! Is this what I got to look forward to? I'm going to have a son who lies to me and goes out on the streets all night?"

"Mama," I said, "Tyrone is alive!"

"I don't care if Tyrone is raised from the dead!" she said. "You were supposed to go get ice cream and no place else!"

Tyrone had been trying to hide behind me, which is stupid because he is about twice as big as I am. But all of a sudden he squatted down and said, "Hey, Ritzi, look what I found on the street when I was chasing those punks."

He pulled something out of his pocket. It was a Barbie with no arm and no leg. Ritzi's eyes got real big. She grabbed the doll and sat down on the floor and started examining it.

Mama said, "Well, look at that. Tyrone found your doll, Ritzi. Can you thank him?"

Ritzi looked up at Tyrone with this expression that if he wasn't my best friend, I would be jealous because she's *my* sister.

"She's okay," said Ritzi.

"Sure she's okay," said Tyrone. "I took good care of her."

Then Mama said, "Tyrone, what happened to your face?" The cut on his cheek was purple colored with dried blood. "No, don't tell me. I don't want to hear. But we have to wash it."

She went and got a washcloth and started washing Tyrone's face. I said, "We found evidence that Ritzi didn't kill the gerbil."

"Of course Ritzi didn't kill the gerbil! She's not going to court, Marco, she's a little girl! Were you all the way over to school? Is that where you went?" She was getting mad again, and she rubbed too hard and Tyrone jumped.

"You have to listen, Mama. It's that teacher, Mrs. Rettle. She leaves open the window to her class, and the cat goes in!"

"So?" said Mama.

"And there is food on the floor left out, like someone is feeding the cats!"

Ritzi said, "Big Boss had better not kill any more of our gerbils. Once he even tried to get the rabbit."

Tyrone and I looked at each other.

"Ritzi, are you saying you knew all along it was Big Boss that killed the gerbil?"

"He had his paw in the cage and I chased him out, but it was too late."

I couldn't believe it. She knew all the time.

"Who saw it besides you?" asked Mama.

"I don't know. I think just me."

"Why didn't you tell someone? Did you tell the teacher? Did you tell the principal? I can't believe this. They are accusing my little girl of killing animals, and no one even bothered to ask her what happened—"

"She ran away too soon," I said.

Mama was really mad now, and when my mother is mad, it's like she has disco lights flashing in her eyes. She started waving the washcloth in the air. "I am calling that principal at home," she said. "I want that teacher fired—"

"Rotten Rettle," I said softly, and Mama didn't even tell me to be polite because *she* knew Mrs. Rettle was rotten too.

Mama went straight to the phone and tried to call Mrs. Gates, but we didn't know where she lived and there must have been a hundred Gateses in the phone book. "Monday morning," said Mama. "Oh boy, am I going to go in there on Monday morning! I am not going to have that woman accusing my child!"

It was great; she was going to take care of everything. And even though it wasn't a court, I figured I would have to go in with my evidence, and that would mean missing workbooks on Monday morning. Maybe I wouldn't have to go to class until it was time for play rehearsal!

Mama decided she would go get the ice

cream. I was grounded for the rest of the night. She also told Tyrone to stay for ice cream.

When she was gone, I said we had to call Mr. Marshan so he would know the head was okay. Tyrone made a face, but he agreed. We knew Mr. Marshan was in the phone book, because we looked him up once. We were going to call and make some stupid joke like Is your refrigerator running? But that time we got scared and hung up.

"You talk, Marco," said Tyrone. "You tell him I have the head."

A little tiny kid's voice answered. "Hewwo?"

"This is Marco. Is Mr. Marshan there?" The little voice didn't say anything. I said to Tyrone, "It's his little kid."

Tyrone said, "Let me hear, let me hear!"

"There's nothing to hear, just breathing and old-fashioned music."

Then I heard some footsteps, and a deeper voice said, "Hello? Hello?"

"Mr. Marshan?" I said. "This is Marco."

"Why, hello, Marco," he said. "How nice to hear from you."

"Tyrone and I have the Monster head,

Mr. Marshan. It's not broken or anything. It's at my house."

"Have you got Tyrone there too?" he asked. "Put Tyrone on the phone."

"Sure, Mr. Marshan, but I want to tell you, it was me and Tyrone both who borrowed it. It wasn't just Tyrone; it was me, too."

He didn't say anything for a few seconds. "Are you sure about that, Marco?"

"Yes sir," I said. "It was both of our faults together."

Tyrone was shaking his head *No, no,* but when he got on, all he said was "Yeah, yeah," and "Yeah, I promise." Then he hung up. "I have to leave the head here," he said. "It can't go outside of your house."

I asked, "Are you still in the play?"

"I think so. Mr. Marshan said, 'Three Strikes and You're Out.'"

"So what number strike is this?"

Tyrone looked confused. "He didn't tell me. I think maybe he's only counting fighting strikes."

I didn't think he'd ever said that before, but maybe he had special rules for the play.

Tyrone said, "I can't show my mother. I have to wait and surprise her when she comes to the play."

Mama came back with the ice cream, and Ritzi put No-Arm in a chair at the table. Tyrone and I put the Monster head in a chair too, but not too close so it wouldn't get dirty.

"Now you got five children, Mama," I said. "Me and Ritzi and Tyrone and old ugly No-Arm and the Main Monster head!"

The only kind of ice cream Uncle Albert had in his freezer that night was the three-flavor kind—strawberry, chocolate, and vanilla. That was fine with us, though, because Ritzi only likes vanilla, and Mama chose just strawberry, so Tyrone and I got all three kinds plus extra chocolate.

8

THE MAIN MONSTER AND HIS MOTHER

On Monday Mama went to school and had a big meeting with Mrs. Gates and Mrs. Rettle. I wanted to go, but it turned out they didn't need me because Rotten Rettle admitted she let in the cats. She said she always takes care of poor stray cats because nobody else does.

Then she quit. Just like that. I don't know if she got scared of my mother, or if Mrs. Gates gave one of her special looks. But she got her stuff and walked out. Mrs. Gates took care of the kindergarten that day.

Ritzi's good teacher got special permission from her doctor to come back early. She had a crutch, but the children all promised to be good. They drew pictures and had a funeral for the dead gerbil.

Meanwhile, we were having our last week of rehearsals. It was time for the Performance! Or I should say the Two Performances, one for the school, and one at night for the parents.

We did nothing else all that week. Mr. Marshan would assign some work, and Lateesha would say, "Oh, Mr. Marshan, I'm worried about the part where the Monster and Cool Girl dance!" Or Robert would say, "Hey, Mr. Marshan, I don't think the Monster Posse knows the song yet."

Mr. Marshan would rub his beard and say, "Well, maybe we should take a break and run through that part again."

The last three days we worked in the auditorium the whole time. It would have been nothing but fun, except for Tyrone getting another strike. Tyrone was acting silly and big-headed about being the star of the show, and Robert said something about his mother.

Nobody talks about Tyrone's mother. The Monster Posse was up on stage waiting to dance while Mr. Marshan found the place on the tape recorder. All of a sudden, *wham!* Tyrone was pounding on Robert. Nobody even heard what Robert said. Robert's mask went *zoom!* across the floor and the Main Monster head got all cockeyed on Tyrone.

Mr. Marshan was there in an instant. He jumped up on the stage like an acrobat and pulled them apart. He put Tyrone on one side of the auditorium and Robert on the other.

When it was quiet again, Mr. Marshan said, "You know what it means if you get into a fight. You know it means a strike." I held my breath. We still weren't sure how many strikes Tyrone had on him. He *couldn't* throw Tyrone out of the play. He just couldn't.

"Robert," he said, "this is Strike One on you. You know what that means. Three Strikes and You're Out." But nobody cared about Robert; he was just one of the Monster Posse monsters. We could lose six of them and the play would still go on. Then he turned to Tyrone.

"Tyrone," he said, "this is getting serious now. You're a good Main Monster, Tyrone, but I swear I will throw you out if you fight. Do you hear me, Tyrone? You got Strike One when you fought Marco. This is Strike Two on you, Tyrone. Three Strikes and You're Out."

I almost cheered! He wasn't counting when Tyrone borrowed the head over the weekend!

"Now, class," said Mr. Marshan. "This is for everyone. Tyrone has a problem with getting strikes. Are we going to let him get Strike Three and get out of the play?"

Everyone except Robert shouted, "No!"

Mr. Marshan said, "It's going to take everyone's help. It's going to take Tyrone most of all, but it takes all of you. Robert, do you hear that? Marco?"

"Yes sir, Mr. Marshan!" I said.

Tyrone promised too.

My friend Tyrone could really act. He was such a good monster! He was good not only when the Monster runs around and threatens people, but also when the Monster loses Cool Girl and gets sad. Tyrone's whole body drooped low.

The next day he was as good as an angel. He did his work in class. He smiled if someone bumped him. He stayed away from Robert. But the day after that, which was the day before the play, he started acting stupid again. On the playground he tried to pinch Miriam. He was lucky she was faster than he was. She said she wasn't going to tell Mr. Marshan, but if he did it again, she'd report him.

In the lunchroom he started growling at the little kids.

"Come on, Tyrone, don't be stupid," I said.

"Yeah, Tyrone," said Robert. "Don't be stupid."

"Who's stupid?" said Tyrone. "Are you calling me stupid?"

I said, "Tyrone, tomorrow's the play." I was worried because Mr. Marshan was on lunch duty, and he could see everything we were doing.

"Okay, okay," said Tyrone.

Just then a little first-grade boy walked by, and Tyrone growled at him. Tyrone just couldn't help himself. The little kid jumped three feet in the air. Tyrone laughed like a crazy hyena, and Robert said to the kid beside him, "I'm telling you, sometimes Tyrone is a regular Mental."

Tyrone growled at Robert.

"Hey, Tyrone," Robert said, "nobody in your family is coming to see you in the play anyhow. Your daddy isn't going to be here because he's—"

"Yeah," said Tyrone, interrupting him, "and your daddy isn't going to be here because your mama doesn't even know his name."

Robert got a look on his face, and I knew he was going to say something about Tyrone's mother. So I screamed, "Shut up, Robert! Watch out, Tyrone! Don't get the Third Strike!"

But it was too late. Robert said, "Tyrone, your mama's not coming because she wears

Kleenex boxes for shoes, and they all wore out!"

I could see it coming. Tyrone hit his milk carton with his fist and started around the table after Robert. I jumped in the way so he couldn't hit him, and then—*crash!*—his elbow hit me in the face! I saw little shiny splashes of light just like the stars when somebody gets knocked out in the cartoons. But I held on to Tyrone! Even when I was hit, I held on to his arm, and when he realized he hit me, he said, "Marco, Marco, are you all right?"

Mr. Marshan came running over, and my eye was hurting so bad I couldn't open it, but I said, "Hey, Mr. Marshan, this is so funny, me and Tyrone, we were practicing our parts, you know where he chases the Narrator, and he threw his arms way out and *wham!* Right in my eye!"

Robert is stupid sometimes, but he would never rat on you. He said, "Yeah, Mr. Marshan, it was pretty funny!"

Mr. Marshan looked like he knew something was going on, but he just said, "Can you open that eye, Marco? I think you better take a walk and go see the nurse."

He sent Tyrone with me and made Robert clean up the spilled milk.

"Are you okay, Marco?" asked Tyrone as we walked down the hall.

"I'm okay, Tyrone, but I'm not going to be okay if you get yourself thrown out of the play."

"I know you're trying to save me, Marco," he said. "I know the whole class is trying to help except for that banana brain Robert. But it's no use. Something always happens to me. Something is going to go wrong and I won't get to do it."

"All you have to do is not get into any fights and show up tomorrow. It's only till tomorrow! The Show Must Go On, Tyrone."

"It's easy for you," he said. "You don't get into fights. But me, I don't even know how it happens. I'm like the Monster: all of a sudden, I'm bad. And I don't think my mama is going to come anyhow."

"Uncle Albert will be there," I said. "You know Uncle Albert watches out for you. And

Ritzi is talking to everybody about how Tyrone is going to be in the play."

He half-smiled. "Does Ritzi talk about me?"

"She never says, 'Oh, my brother is going to be in the play.' It's always, 'Tyrone is going to be in the play!' It's a good thing she's such a little jerk, because I would be jealous."

"Naw," said Tyrone, "you wouldn't be jealous of me." But he smiled, and I thought, Well, we still have a chance.

The next morning on the way to school, Tyrone said, "Hey, Marco, you don't have to take care of me today. I don't have the Monster head on today."

I had had another bad morning getting Ritzi to stop playing Barbies. "So how come you aren't going to fight today?" I asked. "How come today is different?"

He shrugged. "Today I don't put on the Monster till I put on the Monster, if you know what I mean."

"That doesn't make any sense, Tyrone," said Ritzi.

Tyrone just grinned. "Are you coming to the play, Little Ritz? Is your whole class coming?" But of course we already knew the answer to that. *Everyone in the whole school was coming.*

Our room was buzzing like all the bugs in the park in spring. Everything was going crazy. Lateesha screamed that her mind was a blank! She didn't remember a single line! Then someone stepped on one of the masks and broke off a horn. And then Miriam couldn't find her dress, and then my breath got funny in my chest.

All of a sudden it was time to go to the auditorium. Everything sort of smoothed out then. Miriam's dress was in the bottom of her bag after all. The monster mask looked even uglier with one horn than with two. Lateesha's lines all came back, and I could breathe again.

We lined up with all our stuff, very quiet, and very quiet we walked to the auditorium. Kids looked at us from their classrooms. The auditorium was totally silent with just the danger lights on, and the spotlight on the red curtain.

Backstage we set up our stuff. Then things went faster and faster. Our first Performance was about to start!

"Okay, Marco," said Mr. Marshan. "As soon as Mrs. Gates is finished, you go right out."

Mrs. Gates's voice was booming out of the microphone, and you could hear the teachers shushing the kids. Mrs. Gates said something I couldn't understand, and they started clapping.

"Go out, Marco!" said Lateesha.

"Go on, Marco!" said Tyrone.

Mr. Marshan gave me a push.

The spotlight was on just me alone. The microphone worked, and my voice reached all the way to the back of the auditorium.

That was how it started. And the little kids loved the whole thing! I was glad I was the Narrator because I was out there and I could see it all happen.

I could see Lateesha and Miriam and the other girls dance like professionals. I saw the Monster dance, and it was great! When Tyrone made his entrance, he stumbled and almost fell. But he just acted like it was on purpose. He even stumbled again and pretended he was going to fall off the stage! The little kids in the front row practically climbed out of their chairs.

And then came the best part, when the Monster chases the Narrator—me!—out into the auditorium. It was Pandemonium! Some little kids grabbed for Tyrone, and he growled and grabbed back at them. We got it going so good that we ran around the auditorium twice instead of once.

When the Performance was over, and we were all back in our room, we couldn't stop. We kept running around the room and acting out the best parts again. Mrs. Gates came in to say congratulations, and Mr. Marshan warned us to save some energy for the night's performance. To quiet us down, he brought out two big boxes of donuts. But it didn't work. We acted out the best parts for each other and ate donuts at the same time.

That night at dinner, Ritzi kept jumping up and down and telling Mama the story. "And then the Monster ran after the Cool Girl!" she said. "And then the Monster ran after Marco!"

"Okay, Ritzi," said Mama, "eat your dinner or you stay home with the baby-sitter instead of seeing the play again."

Tyrone and I had to go to school early to get things ready. For the Night Performance, Mrs. Allen the secretary had made programs with all our names in them and Mr. Marshan had his camcorder set up on a tripod. I had to wear my sport jacket, but right before the audience started to come in, Mr. Marshan said, "Hey, Marco, here's something for you." And he lent me his tie with the red-and-green parrot. Mr. Marshan and Lateesha's father and even Uncle Albert wore sport jackets too, so I wasn't the only one.

Right before they let all the people in, Tyrone sneaked down to the front row and put his coat on a seat for his mother. He kept sticking his face out between the curtains to make sure nobody took the seat.

"I promised I'd save her a seat in the front row," he said.

I kept my mouth shut, but everyone knew

that Tyrone's mother *never ever* comes to school. Tyrone's mother does not send cupcakes or join the PTA. She does not even come to school when Tyrone gets suspended. That's how often she doesn't come to school.

Mr. Marshan kept telling us to get backstage, but we all kept peeking. The whole auditorium was full. People were standing in the back. The little kids had liked it so much, they all came again, even the ones who didn't have brothers or sisters in the play.

The noise got louder and louder, and we were getting more and more excited. Tyrone kept looking out through the curtains even after Mr. Marshan stopped the rest of us. "Come on, Tyrone," he said. "This is very unprofessional! Tyrone! Get away from the curtain."

"It's too crowded out there," said Tyrone. "I have to watch my coat."

I said, "I wanted my dog Lucy to see the play, but Mama said no way."

"Lucy is just a dog," he said.

Just like the Day Performance, it seemed like it would never start, and then it happened so fast. The audience was a big huge roar, and then—quiet. Mrs. Gates said something about how hard we had worked, and then there was clapping.

I stepped out through the curtain. It was better than magic, the way they got even quieter for me. This was not like the little kids, who kept whispering while the teachers told them to shut up. This was the biggest silence I ever felt. And I was inside it, like inside the mouth of a whale.

I said into the microphone, "Good evening, ladies and gentlemen," but my voice had a squeak in it.

I cleared my throat and took a deep breath and said it again. "Good evening, ladies and gentlemen. Welcome to our play, 'Cool Girl and the Main Monster'—"

Just as I said that, there was a noise in the back of the auditorium, and a voice as loud as me said, "Excuse me! Excuse me! I have a seat in the front!"

And here came this lady with very high heels and a tight red dress with feathery stuff on the top. She had so much hair it was like a volcano coming out the top and down the sides of her head. She came straight to the front row, and I almost said, Excuse me, lady, that is for Tyrone's mother. But then I realized—it *was* Tyrone's mother! I just had never seen her with so much hair before.

The curtain moved behind me. Tyrone stuck his head out. "You see!" he whispered. "I told you she'd come."

So finally the play got started for real. It was just as good as for the little kids—maybe even better, because the audience clapped every time something good happened and nobody had to tell them to shut up in the quiet parts.

Afterward nobody would leave! Mama and Ritzi and Uncle Albert and Mr. Marshan and Mrs. Gates and Lateesha's father and Miriam's parents and Robert's grandmother and all the teachers stayed and stayed.

Mrs. Gates and the PTA had a Reception for us in the gym. There was punch and cookies and coffee. The little kids ran around playing Monster, and one little tiny boy even got up on a chair and pretended he was the Narrator.

I didn't see Tyrone anywhere. I thought maybe his mother took him home or something, but then, all of a sudden, here came Tyrone's mother in her red dress and beside her in a white suit like for a wedding was Tyrone.

Everyone went over to them and said congratulations. Mama and Uncle Albert went over too, and while they were talking, Tyrone and I stood together. I felt shy; he was so fancy in those clothes. "Where did you get that suit?" I said.

"My mother got it for me," he said. "She took me to a store yesterday after school, and they measured my legs and did a special rush job to get it ready and everything."

We stayed quiet for a little while. Then he said, "You know what I like about acting, Marco? When I was the Monster, it was like the Monster took me over. But when you're acting, you can get rid of it when you want to."

"So let's be actors, Tyrone," I said. "We'll make our own movies and act all the parts ourselves."

He grinned. "And everybody will want to be us!"

"Especially us," I said. "We'll want to be us most of all."

So then we went and had chocolate-chip cookies and punch with ice cream floating in it.

And the PTA gave us our punch in real glass cups because we were the stars of the play.